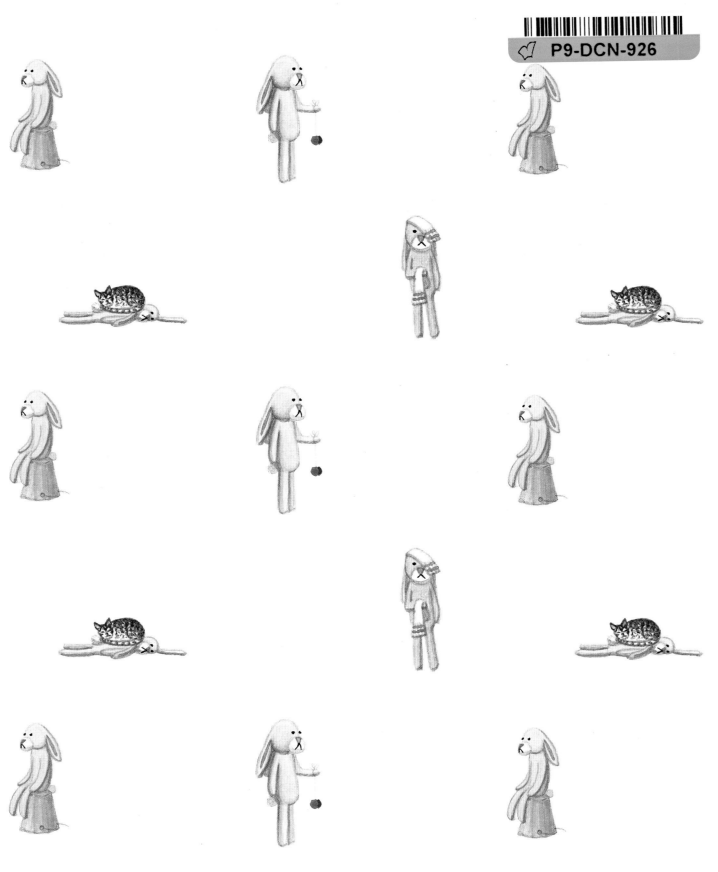

To Franny and Henry with all my love,
and to backups everywhere.—A. R.

For my wife, Brooke.—G. S.

Text copyright © 2018 by Abigail Rayner.
Illustrations copyright © 2018 by Greg Stones.
First published in the United States, Great Britain, Canada, Australia, and New Zealand in 2018
by NorthSouth Books, Inc., an imprint of NordSüd Verlag AG, CH-8050 Zürich, Switzerland.

Distributed in the United States by NorthSouth Books, Inc., New York 10016.
Library of Congress Cataloging-in-Publication Data is available.
ISBN: 978-0-7358-4282-3
Printed in Printed in Latvia by Livonia Print, Riga, 2017.
1 3 5 7 9 · 10 8 6 4 2
www.northsouth.com

The Backup Bunny

by Abigail Rayner

pictures by Greg Stones

North
South

I guess you're wondering what a luxury stuffed rabbit like me is doing in Mom's sock drawer.

I'm the backup bunny.

What's the backup bunny, you ask?

If Max ever loses his favorite stuffed rabbit,
I step in to save the day.

Simple.

Or it should be.

Let me tell you about the time that Max lost Bunny.
For months, I had waited.

I dreamed about what it would
be like to be played with.

And then, it happened.

One night, I was yanked from
the sock drawer. Max was crying,
and I was pressed into his arms.

My chance to save the day, and be loved by a child.
Or so I thought.

Max squeezed me. He pressed me to his cheek.
He petted the tips of my ears.
For a second, I was truly happy.

And then . . .

SPLAT!

"That's **NOT** Bunny!" shouted Max.
"His ears don't feel right!"
Mom put me back in his bed.
Max threw me out.

This went on for a while.

At least the cat liked me.

The next day, we went for a bike ride

and to the grocery store

and to art class.

"I may not be Bunny, but I am A bunny,"
I said as I hung by my ears from the
clothesline. "I deserve some respect!"

That was when I saw
him. BUNNY. He was
slumped over the edge
of the tree house.

I decided not to mention it.
This was my chance.

I couldn't go back to the sock drawer yet.

I decided to free myself from the clothesline.
I tugged, I wriggled, and I hopped. Finally, I fell.
Straight into Max's mud pie.

"Oh great!"

But Max didn't throw me.
He giggled. He sat me on a bucket
and made me a snack.

Later, we rode his bike, and swung, and played dress-up.

"Are you sure I look good in this?"

I couldn't have been happier.

Unless . . .

But at bedtime, when Mom
tucked me into Max's bed . . .

"I want Bunny!"

THUD!

"Hey! I'm a luxury rabbit with extra-long ears who is guaranteed to be your friend for life!"

"I just want Bunny!" said Max.

It was no use. Max was my friend and I couldn't bear to see him sad. "You want to know where Bunny is? You left him in the tree house."

Max stopped crying. "Mama! I remember where I left Bunny."

So here I am. Back in the sock drawer.

With the Christmas socks ...

... the socks with holes in them,
and the sad single socks. It's where I belong.

"**Yeesh!** When's the last time you guys had a bath?"

WAAAAAH!

"Wait! What's happening?"
"Did Max lose Bunny again?"

"But he's right there, under your arm!"

"WAAAAH!"

"I want the other bunny too—
the **FLUFFY** one," shouted Max.

"You mean you want . . .
" . . . ME?"

Now I go everywhere with Max and Bunny. Except when Max is forgetful.

"Hey! I'm under here!
Move, you stinking purr machine!
I am NOT your cushion."

"Wait! Who is THAT guy?"